Good Boy, Fergus!

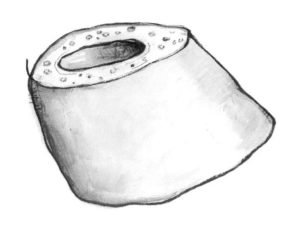
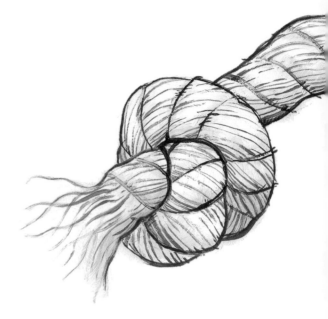
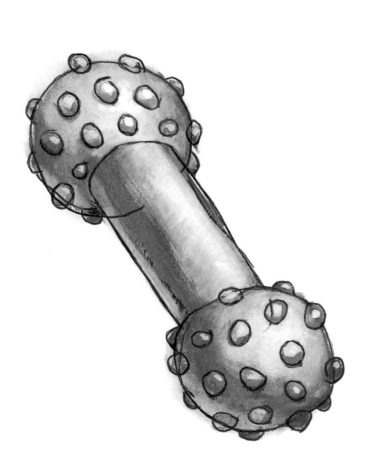

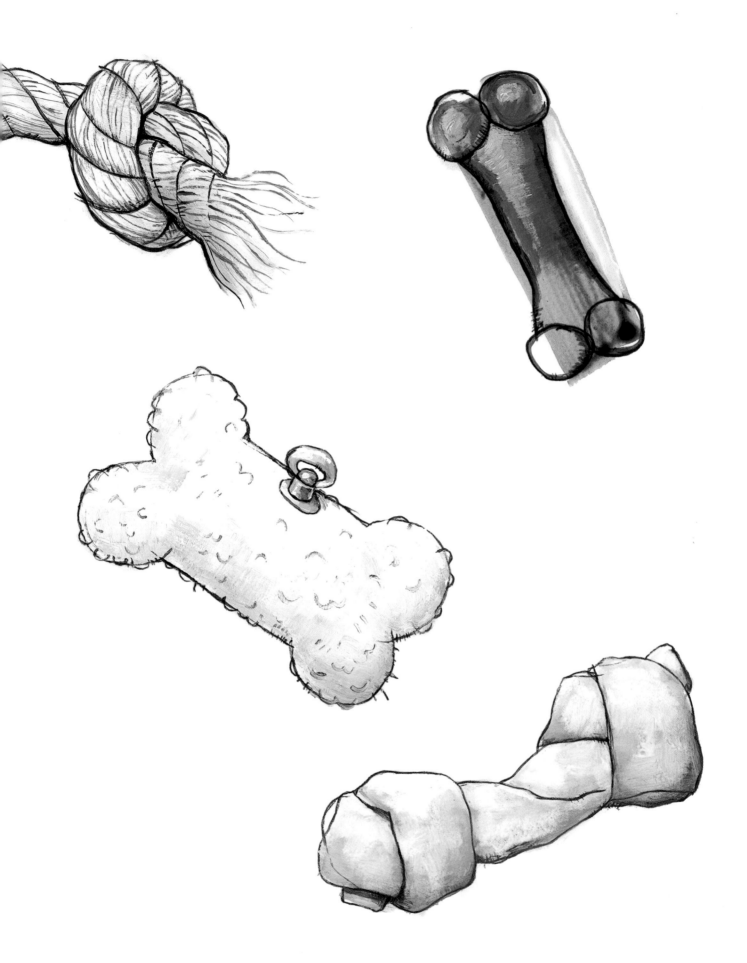

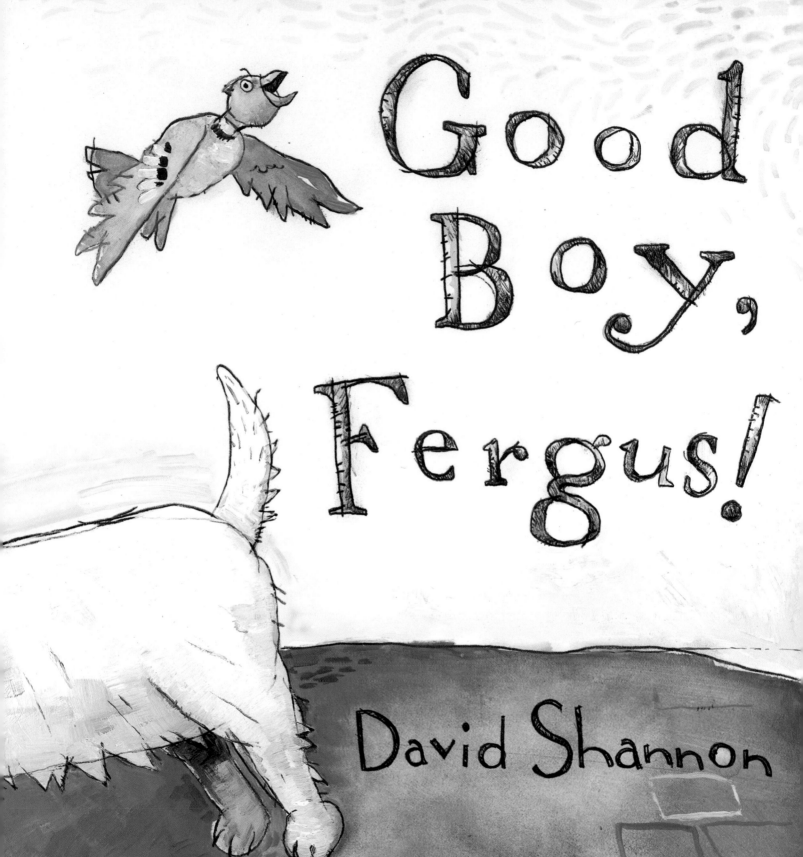

Good Boy, Fergus!

David Shannon

SCHOLASTIC INC.
New York Toronto London Auckland Sydney
Mexico City New Delhi Hong Kong Buenos Aires

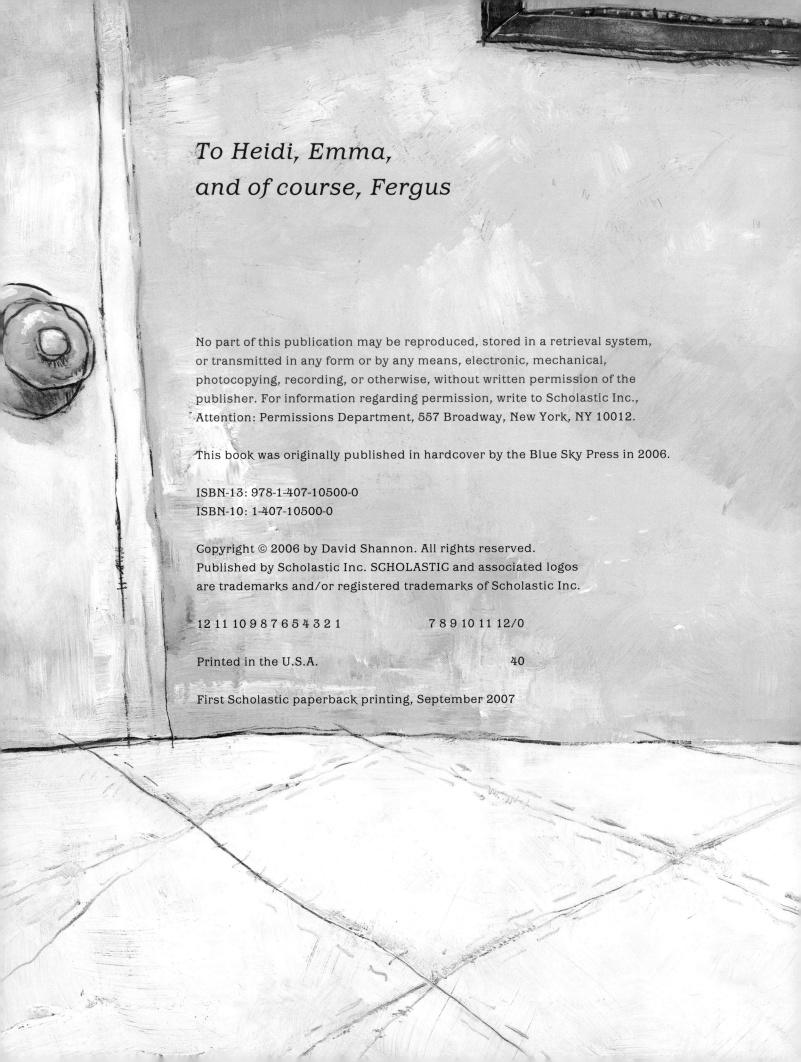

To Heidi, Emma,
and of course, Fergus

This book was originally published in hardcover by the Blue Sky Press in 2006.

ISBN-13: 978-1-407-10500-0
ISBN-10: 1-407-10500-0

12 11 10 9 8 7 6 5 4 3 2 1   7 8 9 10 11 12/0

Printed in the U.S.A.   40

First Scholastic paperback printing, September 2007

Ready...

set...

Okay, Fergie, time to go in. Come here, Ferg. C'mon boy. FERGUS, COME! Here Fe Fergie, Fergie! MACLAGGA HERE RIGHT NO come on. Let's

Good boy, Fergus!

It's
Mr. F!

Mister
itchy bobo
scratchitty
man!

Sit. Fergus.

Down.

Roll over.

Good boy, Fergus!

Bath time!

Now let's go for a ride!

Don't beg, Fergus.

Oh, all right...

Good boy, Fergus!

Time

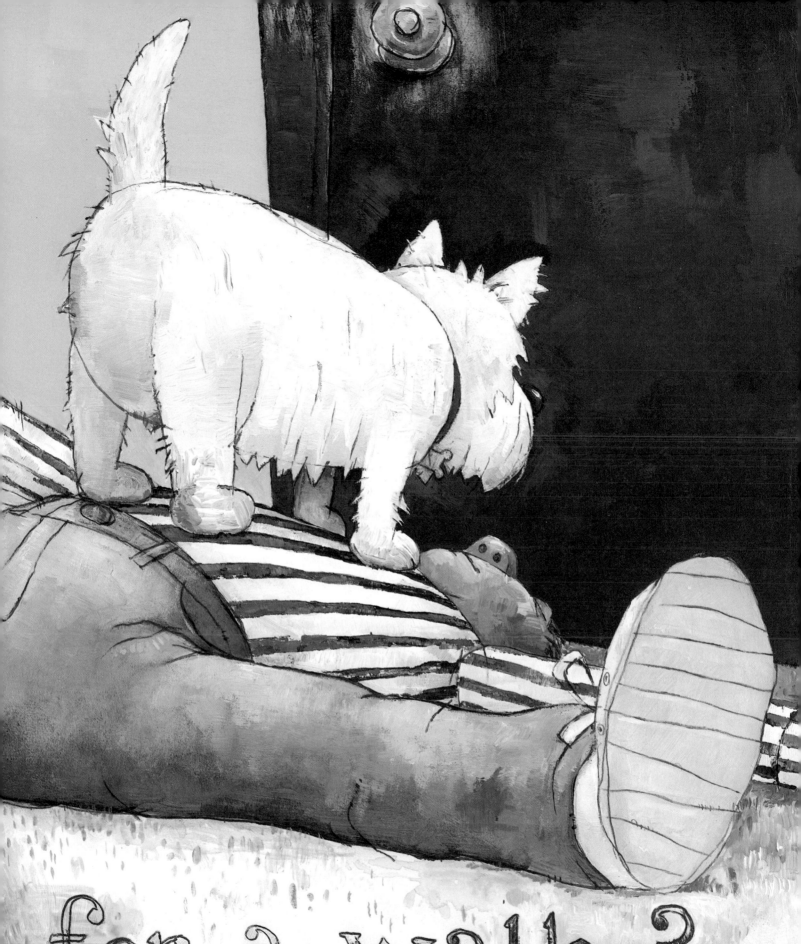

for a walk ?

DINNER TIME!

Bet

What's the problem?

Sweet dreams,
little Fergus.

Good boy.

David Shannon

is the award-winning illustrator
of more than twenty books for children,
and *Good Boy, Fergus!* is the tenth book
he has also written himself. His most
recent picture book, *Alice the Fairy* (2004),
was a *New York Times* bestseller and a
Book Sense finalist. His many awards
include a Caldecott Honor for his beloved
No, David!, which was followed by two more
bestselling "David" picture books: *David
Gets in Trouble* and *David Goes to School*.
He lives in Southern California with his wife,
Heidi, their daughter, Emma, and their
West Highland terrier, Fergus. If you look
closely, you'll find Fergus in ten of
David Shannon's books.

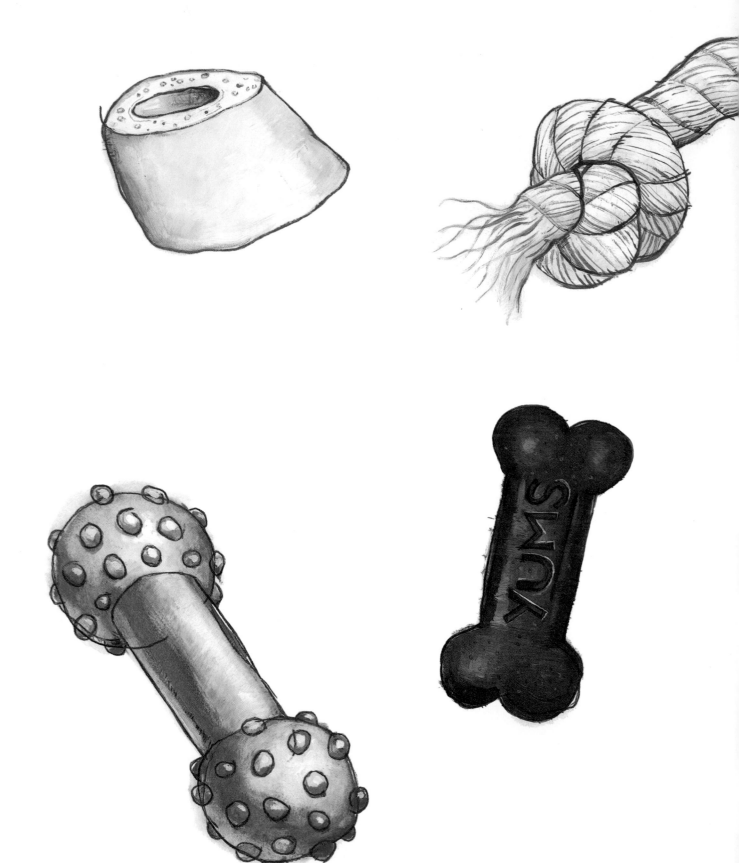

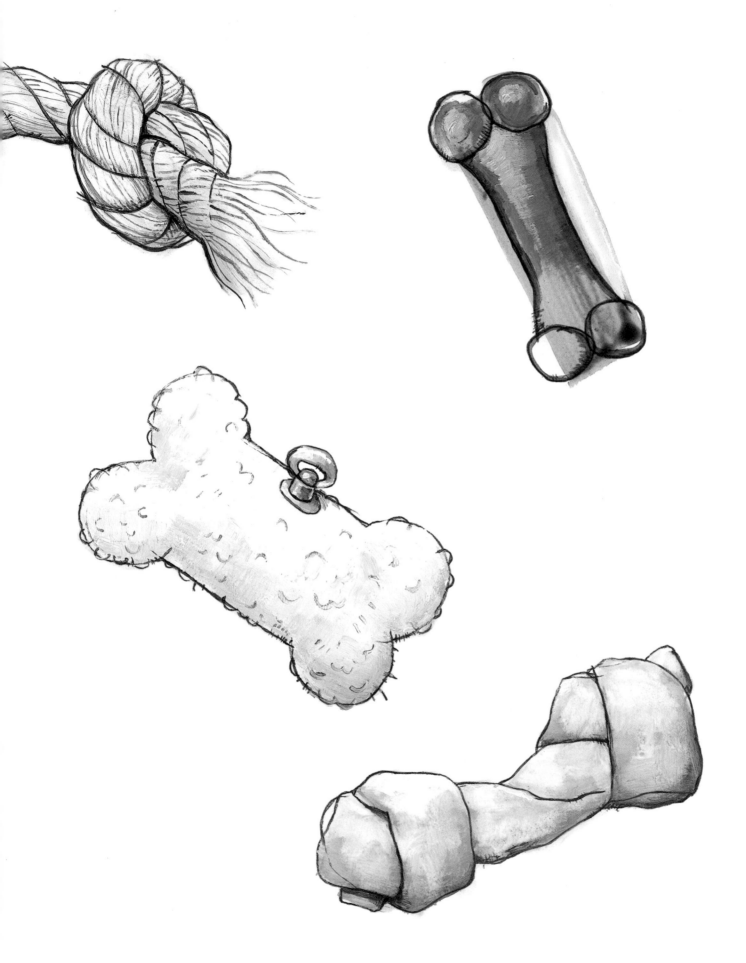